MARK J

Illustrated by
Peter Melnyczuk

OXFORD
UNIVERSITY PRESS

For Sarah and Nichola Rudolf
my keen critics and very good friends
for many years

OXFORD
UNIVERSITY PRESS

Great Clarendon Street, Oxford OX2 6DP

Oxford University Press is a department of the University of Oxford.
It furthers the University's objective of excellence in research, scholarship,
and education by publishing worldwide in

Oxford New York

Athens Auckland Bangkok Bogotá Buenos Aires Cape Town
Chennai Dar es Salaam Delhi Florence Hong Kong Istanbul Karachi
Kolkata Kuala Lumpur Madrid Melbourne Mexico City Mumbai Nairobi
Paris São Paulo Shanghai Singapore Taipei Tokyo Toronto Warsaw

and associated companies in Berlin Ibadan

Oxford is a trade mark of Oxford University Press
in the UK and in certain other countries

British Library Cataloguing in Publication Data
Data available

ISBN 0 19 915962 9

Printed in the UK by Ebenezer Baylis & Son Ltd

Available in packs

Year 5 / Primary 6 Pack of Six (one of each book)   ISBN 0 19 915963 7
Year 5 / Primary 6 Class Pack (six of each book)   ISBN 0 19 915964 5

Contents

South Pacific
Ocean

Quito

ANDES

Amazon
Rainforest

ECUADOR

Chapter One

The sun baked down on the dense green trees, crowding both sides of the drive. Oranges and lemons hung from their branches, avocados too, the size of grapefruit back home.

"Hang on a minute, Jack." Sammy trailed behind me as though he was sleepwalking – no wonder after the endless flight and the long bumpy drive.

I reached the muddy pot-holed track, which Uncle Don called the "main road", and stopped to wait for him.

Ecuador! South America! I've never even been abroad before – Mum and Dad don't have time for holidays – and it still didn't quite seem real.

Uncle Don and Aunt Clara live in a valley on the Eastern slopes of the Andes. My mates at school have been to Spain and Greece and that, but nowhere like this. The mountainside ahead was steep as a skyscraper, but ten times higher, and green all the way up. On the drive down here, I'd seen Indian people in tribal costumes, and a real volcano, gushing clouds of ash.

"So, what d'you think she'll be like?" Sammy glanced around, still nervous about four whole weeks away from Mum and Dad. But underneath he was at least as excited as me. He meant our sort-of-cousin, Jody, who, apparently, was swimming in the local river. We'd just got here and we were going down there to say hello.

I'm twelve, Sammy's nine, and Mum

and Dad thought it was great that Jody is eleven, right between us. "What do you think?" I asked him. "She's a *girl*, isn't she?"

I hadn't seen much of girls for a while – the college is boys only, thank goodness. But the ones I remembered from Elmdale Primary were mostly gossips and dobbers. Now Jody would be the only kid for miles who even spoke English.

"But, Jack..." Sammy's still at Elmdale. One of his best mates is a girl.

"Come on." I led on across the road. "Let's go and see."

The river roared along in its rocky bed but just here there was a quieter place, a pool, twenty metres long. A couple of kids splashed around while half a dozen more stood on the bank.

Swimming is my favourite thing, but I mean *swimming*, not messing about in some river. The biggest kid, about fourteen, was perched on top of a huge high rock, as if he was going to dive in. He must be *crazy*. There were more rocks *everywhere*. It would be suicide.

Obviously he realized this. He faffed about, while the others laughed and shouted in Spanish – that's what they talk here – clearly egging him on.

Jody wasn't though.

All the others were boys, brown-skinned, with black hair, wearing old shorts or cut-offs. Jody didn't look that different. It was easy to spot her though, because she was wearing a bright blue swimsuit. While they all shouted at the kid on the rock, she just stood there with hands on hips.

The older boy made the smart move and climbed down. That was what Jody was waiting for. She scrambled up to where he'd been and didn't even hesitate, just plunged in.

"Wow!" Sammy was impressed.

But the seconds passed and Jody didn't surface.

Chapter Two

I ran down to the waterside.

I swim a great freestyle. I was the only Year 7 picked for the junior team last season. I mostly do racing, but I've got my lifesaving certificates. If Jody didn't show I'd have to go in after her.

The boys didn't seem worried, but I started undoing my trainers. Then a head appeared down the far end of the pool. Jody swam over and climbed out. "Oh, hi. You're the guys from England, right?" She didn't seem exactly thrilled to see us.

She was skinny and almost as tall as me,

with a thin face, big dark eyes and a wide nose which turned up slightly.

Maybe I should shake hands, but she was streaming water and it seemed stupid. In the end I just said, "Hi."

"Great dive!" said Sammy.

"You bet. Wanna try?" She had a strong American accent, like her dad, who'd worked in Texas before coming here. She turned to me. "How about you? You do swimming, right?"

"Yeah, *swimming*." I was about to say something about stupid little pools in stupid little rivers and even stupider things to do in them, but I stopped myself. "Haven't got my trunks."

Jody shrugged. "Shame. None of these kids can do it. I mean they don't *dare*." She said something in Spanish – probably taunting the bigger boy. "Last one who tried broke his wrist. Gets a bit tight." She nodded at the shapes of rocks, just centimetres below the surface.

Jody didn't seem anything like those girls at primary school. But that didn't mean she was better. I kept quiet.

"I'm gonna do a couple more dives," she told us. "Hang around if you like." She climbed up onto the big rock and shouted something to the boys.

No way was I going to stand and watch her showing off, so I grabbed Sammy and headed back. He looked disappointed but he was being good today and he didn't make a fuss.

Aunt Clara's house was like an antique shop with lamps and clocks, huge old wooden tables and chairs, and brass pots and pans hanging on the walls.

Uncle Don had rung to say he couldn't make it for dinner. Apparently this was normal, and it beats our house where, half the time, neither Mum nor Dad get in till half-seven. I usually get our dinner from the fridge.

No sign of Jody either.

"She soon be here." Aunt Clara sounded foreign. She was short and plump, with long black hair hanging down behind, wrapped in a funny ribbon thing. She smiled at us, then went off to the kitchen, and came back with steaming plates of steak and rice and chips.

"Sit, boys." She gave Sammy *another* hug before he could dodge. Poor kid gets it all the time, just because he's small and blond and cute. I was taller than Aunt

Clara and not at all cute, so I was OK. "Eat up." Another wide grin.

Jody dashed in just as we started, then spent the entire meal telling us how wonderful she was at basketball, tennis and every other sport you can think of. She thought she was the best at everything, just because she could dive off that stupid rock.

The food was great though. For some reason, Jody smothered hers in hot chilli sauce – more showing off.

"So, what's it like around here?" I asked her when Aunt Clara went off to do the dishes.

"Total dump." Jody acted bored most of the time. "No idea what I'm gonna do with you guys for a month." Really encouraging.

"Are you on holiday?" I tried again.

"Yeah." She yawned. "All July, all August and half September too."

"Where's your school then?"

"Quito. Academia Cotopaxi – the best

in Ecuador. All in English, of course. I stay up with my friends in the week. Can't wait for next term."

I'd got the point. This place was boring and so were we.

"How long have you lived here?" asked Sammy.

"Three years. We used to live in Quito. That was OK – well, at least you got the movies there. I'm gonna go to university in England. I fancied the States, but Dad wants me to go to Cambridge like him." She shrugged. "I guess that'll do. Next year I'm gonna make him send me to boarding school over there too."

Fine, so long as it wasn't within 200 miles of us. What a jerk – thinking *Cambridge* would "do". Only the cleverest people can even get in there.

"I'm gonna do law maybe, or architecture," she went on. "Something where you make lots of money. Or maybe I'll..."

"I'm tired," I broke into the latest ego-trip. "Long journey, you know. I think we'll have an early night."

"Oh, OK." Jody took us upstairs to a plain little room with two comfortable beds.

It was only eight o'clock, but it was completely dark, even in August. Of course Ecuador is right on the equator – that's where the name comes from – and it gets dark at six-thirty, all year round.

Sammy was asleep in about five seconds, but I couldn't stop thinking about Jody. Four weeks, and we'd be expected to hang out with her the whole time. Ecuador or no Ecuador, how was I ever going to stand it?

Chapter Three

It didn't get any better.

Next day, Jody took us to see "the village": half a dozen wooden shacks on each side of the road. One said "Restaurante". Another might be a shop. It looked as though a good gust of wind would blow them all away.

Then she spotted some boys playing volleyball. Apparently the girls round here don't do sport or swim in the river or anything like that. All Jody's friends were boys. She made us join the game. In fact, we had to take them on, never mind that

Sammy and I had never played before. Of course we got thrashed. Of course it was a nightmare.

Jody had a great time though. I have to admit she was as good as any of the boys, maybe better. And having team-mates who couldn't play gave her the perfect chance to show off.

When we got back, she and Sammy spent hours in the garden, banging a volleyball around. Supposedly she was teaching him to play.

I just read my book until, in the middle of the afternoon, Uncle Don's big four-wheel drive roared in.

Uncle Don is huge, with blue eyes, a curly brown bush of hair and a big reddish beard. "Hi there, guys." He's not really my uncle, but Dad's best friend from university. "So, you ready for the big expedition tomorrow?"

Jody groaned, and, for once, I had to agree with her. This was Uncle Don's big idea, camping in the forest. Problem was, the forest around here grew on the mountains and any expedition was going to be straight up.

But Mum and Dad had thought it sounded great, and the whole thing was fixed over the phone, before anyone even told me. At least Sammy was looking forward to it.

"Great time to go," said Uncle Don. "I have to be up in Quito for a few days, see, so I won't be here to run you guys around." As if he'd done any "running around" whatsoever. We'd hardly seen him.

"Hang on," I said. "You mean you're not coming with us?"

He winked. "Can't this time, but you're gonna love it. You get great views down towards the Amazon."

Was that *it*? We'd had *views* on the drive down here.

"You'll be fine, but listen." Uncle Don's face got very serious. "It's perfectly safe, so long as you know what you're doing. Jody's been up loads of times, right, pumpkin?" He winked at his daughter, who made a face.

"I *told* you not to call me that."

"So," he went on, "up there, she's boss. You gotta do just what she says, OK?"

I couldn't believe it. I'm older, bigger *and* I'm a boy. He couldn't put me in charge, as I've never been in this forest but, oh, why did we have to have leaders and stuff? As if Jody wasn't bossy enough.

But, as usual, everything was settled. We were taking a tent and cooking our own food. All I know about that stuff is "microwave on high for three minutes", so it would be a joke unless Jody knew how. We were supposed to spend three days up there.

Three *days* – what a nightmare!

At least this was a chance to show off some stuff I'd read. "Hey," I told them, when Uncle Don had gone, "maybe we'll find Atahualpa's treasure."

Jody screwed up her face. "*What?*"

But Sammy grinned. "Let's look for it. What is it?"

"The last Inca King," I told them. "Atahualpa and his brother had a civil war. That's how come the Spanish took over so easily. He had all this..."

"I know that stuff," snorted Jody. "I *live* here, remember. Anyway, you're wrong. There were less than 200

Spaniards, and Atahualpa had 40,000 men. The real reason they lost..."

Here we went again. I'd read this stuff in a book, but Jody had to know better.

"You know," she went on, "like the year 2000, all those crazies predicting the end of the world. Same thing back then, but the Incas took it seriously. They were *expecting* the world to end. Then the Spanish came. I guess their prediction came true, kind of."

She stared at me as though I was some kind of beetle. "There are lots of stories about Inca treasure, Jack, but you can bet the Spanish got it all. Why would you wanna play some stupid kids' game? Can't we act like adults for once?"

I hadn't meant that at all. Now Sammy was disappointed, and having this eleven-year-old tell me to grow up was just too much. There had to be some way to teach her a lesson.

Chapter Four

"Trainers are fine," said Jody. "Won't be too muddy this time of year."

Just as well. She had leather boots, like hikers wear. For me, hikers are only one step short of crazy. Trainers were all I had.

Jody wore a T-shirt and black shorts and we both had shirts and jeans. A trip like this, we were bound to end up filthy, so I chose my oldest stuff, but Sammy insisted on his new, bright orange T-shirt.

We followed Jody out to the porch. The morning sun hung low, the same colour as the oranges on the trees. Aunt Clara had packed for us last night and – oh, I couldn't believe it.

Sammy had a small day-pack, with just his own stuff. Mine was a normal rucksack with change of clothes, sleeping bag, and some of the food. But Jody's pack was twice as big. She had the tent, all the cooking gear, and a huge machete-knife thing, almost a metre long. It was ridiculous. Obviously I didn't want a load of heavy stuff but I felt insulted – to have a girl carrying everything. She picked it up with no problem though.

"Hey, I can take more than this," I told her.

Jody shrugged. "We're almost 2,000 metres up, here. The air's pretty thin and you guys aren't used to it. I spend most of my time up in Quito at 3,000. Dad always makes me carry my share."

"Hang on, Jody." We hurried after her down the drive. Uncle Don was long gone, so we had to walk along the road to where the trail began. The air seemed fine to me. "That's the point, it's not just your share."

"Oh, let's not argue the whole time. See how you go, OK?"

A few hundred metres down the road, she turned off beside a small stream. A few metres, a bend in the path, and we were in another world. Tree branches formed a ceiling overhead. A wall of undergrowth crowded in, bright with red flowers, like bells hung on a string.

It was like one of those butterfly farms. There were hundreds, all colours, but red and orange were favourite. Black too. Weird colour for a butterfly, but then I saw one land in the shadows and just disappear. Must be camouflage.

Behind us, Sammy squealed.

One of the largest butterflies, black with bands of red, had landed on his shoulder and was just sitting there. "Look! It likes me!"

"It's the shirt," said Jody. "They go for bright colours."

A few hundred metres on we came to a shack, a field of small palm trees – and no more path. Jody got out the long knife and carried on along the stream bank, cutting her way through the undergrowth.

"We were up here a few weeks back." Hard to hear her over the swishing machete. "Gotta do this every time."

There was no sign anyone had been here, ever.

It got steep and Jody took it slowly. No wonder, under that load. I glanced around and Sammy grinned, clearly enjoying himself.

I wasn't, though. It *was* interesting but, oh... I'm pretty fit – I train for swimming all year round, three times a week – but now Jody was carrying everything *and* cutting the path, while I was having more and more problems just keeping up. No point getting upset though. Like she said, she was used to the altitude.

At last we stopped for lunch. Aunt Clara had made cheese and tomato sandwiches, just like back home, though this bread was almost as sweet as sponge cake.

I jumped up – a sudden blaring, right in my ear. A car horn! No, must be a motorbike. But Jody said that no one ever came up here.

Chapter Five

I stared around, heart hammering. Sammy was up too, but Jody sat munching away.

"What was that?" I asked her.

Jody swallowed her mouthful. "Come *on*, guys, it's only a *ching-ching*. What am I going to do with you if you panic at every little thing?"

"A *what*?"

"Bird. You'll never see him in there." She glanced into the bushes, then returned to her sandwich.

I sat down again. "Are there no dangerous animals up here, then?"

"Only snakes."

Oh no! I glanced at Sammy, saw him go pale. If I hadn't been startled by that stupid bird, I'd never have asked something so dumb. Sammy hates snakes – common enough fear, I suppose.

"It's OK." Jody must have noticed too. "There are hardly any poisonous ones, and *we* won't see *any*." She grinned and patted a bare leg. "You can see how worried I am."

Sammy relaxed at once. Why? If I told him that he'd never listen, but he was treating Jody almost like Mum. As though she could never be wrong. I wasn't so sure, but with Sammy's phobia, I wasn't going to argue.

"How many times have you been up here?" I asked her.

"The forest? Loads of times."

"I mean this, er, trail." As if there *was* one. "You know, where your dad said. Where we're going."

She gave me an odd look. "Dad and I camped up here twice."

"What about your mum?" asked Sammy. "Doesn't she come?"

"Oh no, not her thing. She'd come if Dad said so. They hardly ever argue." Jody sounded almost disgusted. "That's how most women are around here." Now she smiled. "Good thing Dad always does what *I* say."

"So," I got back to the point, "you've never been up here on your own – I mean without an adult?"

Jody grinned again. "Sure, that's right."

In the afternoon the forest opened out – more typical, Jody reckoned. Tree trunks soared up, their branches closing off the sky, hung with wisps and strands of grey-green moss. Underfoot, it was mostly short grass, and we didn't need the machete any more. Beneath the thick leaf-canopy, it was like walking underwater, dim and cool and green.

We reached another stream and followed it. We could walk side by side, and I had enough breath for talking now. Maybe because it wasn't so steep. Or maybe I was getting used to it.

"Your mum's stuck out here without a car, then?" I asked Jody. The idea of my mum without a car – she won't walk to the end of the street to post a letter.

Jody glanced at me. "*Car?* She doesn't *drive*. She's a full-blooded Indian, you know."

"You mean like in Westerns?" blurted Sammy.

"Don't be..." I was going to say, don't be stupid, this is *South* America, but Jody was nodding.

"More or less. In the US, white people almost wiped them out. But here almost everyone's either Indian or *mestizo* – mixed race – like me."

She frowned. "Mom doesn't wanna drive, never even tried."

"Are you descended from the Incas?" I asked.

"Mom's Quichua, a mixture, some Inca probably, also Quiucara, the people who were here before. There were rainforest

Indians too – came upriver from Brazil. They all intermarried."

"Does she know stories," asked Sammy, "like about the treasure?"

Jody frowned. "Abuelita – my granny – used to tell me things. Told Mom too, when she was little, but Mom won't talk about it now. She's very religious, Catholic, goes to *church*." She shook her head. "It really gets to me. All this stuff and it just gets wasted."

"What stuff?" I'd lost her drift.

"You know, some guy, the pope, whatever, wants everybody to think the same, so everything else gets lost, just wiped out. And no one cares." She'd never talked like this – something she seemed to care about at least. At *last*.

"Down in the Amazon there were tribes who'd never seen white people, even just a few years back. The missionaries went in – the government actually helped them – and destroyed everything, all their way of life.

Those Indians knew all kinds of things the rest of the world has forgotten, and they just wiped it out."

Jody sighed. "Nowadays they try to preserve the old ways, kind of, but it's mostly for tourists – just a show." She'd never gone on like this and she must have realized because she clammed up completely.

It was kind of interesting and I tried to get her going again, but she'd hardly reply, just walked along, staring at the ground. Then she got the machete out and started whirling it around, cutting down all kinds of things that weren't even in the way.

Try something different. I didn't want to get anywhere near the helicopter-blade machete, so I called from a safe distance. "Is this the original rainforest?"

Jody stopped whirling, stopped altogether, turned and looked at me.

I waved a hand around. "This stuff you're cutting down."

Her familiar scornful face was back. "*Cloud*forest. The *rain*forest is down around the Amazon."

"What's the difference?"

She shook her head as though I was an idiot, then pointed through a gap in the trees on our left. There'd been nothing to see so far. Now there was a narrow view, another mountainside, more forest. Sure enough, clouds wandered amongst the trees, some lower down than we were.

"OK," I said, "but stop splitting hairs. I meant..." Then I realized. This was the first view we'd had, and it wasn't much of one. "Hey, your dad said we'd have views down to the Amazon. What happened to them?"

"Oh, yeah," said Jody. "We're not going that way any more." She turned away and headed up the hill again.

Chapter Six

"Hang on." I hurried after her. "What are you on about?"

"We're going somewhere different."

"Where? Have you been there before?"

"Not really."

"You're *joking*. This is crazy." I stopped, but Jody walked on. So did Sammy, and I had to run to catch them up. I grabbed her shoulder, forced her to stop. "What's the idea? First time up here on your own and you take us somewhere new – what if we get lost?"

She smiled and pointed at the stream.

"What d'you mean?"

"*Obviously* we can follow it down. How can we get lost?" She shook free and started off again.

"Look, wait a minute, will you. If something goes wrong, they won't know where to look for us. Let's go where we're supposed to go, OK?"

Jody grinned. "You wouldn't know where I'm taking you anyway."

"We don't have to come."

"Fine. You gonna find your own way back?"

My turn to point at the stream.

"Jack, I think..." Sammy was getting worried.

"Fine," repeated Jody. "Go for it. Bit of a long way round though."

"Look, stop." I grabbed her arm this time. "Let's just talk about it."

She turned to face me. "Let go."

I did.

"No," she said, "we won't talk about it.

I'm in charge, remember. Now shut up and come on." Off she went again.

And *again* Sammy followed.

Normally I keep my cool pretty well, but with Jody I was starting to forget what cool even meant. I followed for an hour, fuming like that erupting volcano. There was no sign anyone had ever even *tried* to teach her how to act like a reasonable human being. Much more of this and I might give it a go.

But with Sammy around, I couldn't risk starting anything. We had to stay together. I'd just have to make sure she didn't take us anywhere stupid.

Up ahead they were waiting for me, and Jody said something – I don't remember what. I doubt I even heard, I was so angry.

"Don't be a baby, Jack." I heard *that*. "What's the point of sulking?"

"I'm *not* sulking."

"Come on. You are, you know," said Sammy.

I ignored him. "*You* told me to shut up, great leader."

Jody shrugged. "Fine, so talk. For a start you can tell me what you guys are doing out here on your own."

Sammy was going to answer if I didn't, and goodness knew what he'd say. He doesn't really understand.

"It's Mum and Dad," I began as we set off again. "They've got – problems." Why should I tell her about this stuff?

"Like what?"

"Oh, I don't know. They don't really talk to us."

"They just argue all the time," put in Sammy.

"Probably work," I went on. "They work all hours, hardly see each other. They're both taking time off to get things sorted. Didn't want us around to get in the way."

"Gee," said Jody, staring ahead of her, "maybe there's something in the system here, with the women just keeping house. Not me, though. Hey, maybe in England I'll find some *guy* to keep house. What d'ya think?"

"Yeah. In your dreams."

"You don't know. Instead of just *assuming* it's only ever women who wanna stay home, people get to choose now."

I must know ten times more about this stuff than she did, stuck out here, but why argue? I didn't want to talk to Jody, not about *anything*. I dropped behind, left them chatting, no idea what about. Who cared?

It hadn't been that steep for a while. Now it was almost level. Were we getting to the top? It was more open too, and I got more and more glimpses through to endless forest-covered slopes.

Then I saw something that made me stop and stare. Ahead and high above was a fold in the mountains, a narrow valley.

At the top, one huge tree towered above all the rest.

Suddenly, for no reason, I wanted to go up and take a look at that big tree. Not that there'd be much to see. Up close it would be like all the others, just a trunk, heading up into the canopy. A larger trunk maybe, but–

"Come on!" Sammy's voice.

I'd been standing for minutes, just staring at the valley and the tree.

"Actually, we'll stop here." Jody headed back towards me.

I looked around. There was a clearing, enough space for a fire, and plenty of dead wood to burn.

"Come on," she said, "we'll pitch the tent. Hey, you two have done real good. I never thought we'd get *this* far."

It was the first compliment she'd paid either of us. For some reason I was really pleased, and that annoyed me more than anything.

Chapter Seven

This was the best part so far – though that wasn't saying much. It was exciting to be out here on our own and fun putting the tent up and collecting wood. Jody built a fire and stuck two candles underneath to get it lit.

She made a stew with beans, sausages and potatoes – not bad at all. Then we settled down in the tent to sleep.

So dark. So quiet. A cloudforest in the Andes! I had to pinch myself to believe it. I was still angry, still worried about going the wrong way, but I was so tired and relaxed, nothing could keep me awake.

I was walking alone in the forest, up a steep rocky valley with no stream. I felt fine, not tired at all. A breeze stirred the branches and everything smelled fresh, like a wood in England after rain. I was going to walk and walk until – well, I wasn't sure. It didn't matter. It was great.

Someone was walking ahead of me. No one I knew and I never saw him properly, just a shadow in the dim light, a glimpse of a slim brown back or long brown legs. I wanted to overtake him, find out who he was, what he was doing here. But I couldn't catch up. It didn't matter. I followed him, and that was right.

Then came something that wasn't great and wasn't right at all. A sudden flash, a double image, barely seen. First bright, then very red.

I didn't like it, but it wouldn't turn me back. I hurried on. I *had* to get to the top now, whatever might be waiting there.

I opened my eyes and it wasn't quite dark. The dream was still vivid. Apart from that half-seen flash, it was an excellent dream and I turned over to go back to sleep. No use. When a dream's over, that's it.

I got up on one elbow. At the end of the tent, the loose flap stirred in the breeze and daylight spilled in – enough to show that Jody was gone.

I got up, pulled on my clothes, slowly and carefully so I wouldn't wake Sammy, then wriggled out of the tent, like a mole coming up to see the morning. No sign of Jody, but the fire was burning, with a pot of water almost at the boil. I huddled close for warmth against the morning chill.

Cloudforest – now I could really see why. Above my head, just a few metres up, small wisps wandered through the branches, hanging the trailing moss with crystal beads of moisture.

In the distance, something bright shone through the trees. A fire – a *big* fire! I jumped up and looked through a break in the foliage.

It was that huge tree at the top of the little valley, blazing yellow in the first rays of the invisible sun. Could that be the valley I'd walked up in my dream? Somehow it *had* to be.

"Up at last."

I jumped about a mile. "Don't creep up like that!"

Jody grinned. "Hey, I'm just naturally light on my feet. You guys overslept."

I pointed at the tree. "Is that where we're going?"

Her eyes widened. "How did you know?"

"Look, Jody, I don't want to have a row or... Yesterday – if Sammy wasn't here, I'd just have gone back but... What I mean is, couldn't we do what we planned, go where your dad thinks we're going?" Why was I saying this? It wasn't what I wanted, not now. Not at all.

Jody hesitated. "Bit late for that – we're on the wrong mountain. Anyway, I've always wanted to go up there." Her turn to point at the shining tree. "It's not much further."

Weird, as though she felt exactly the same way I did.

"Anyway," she grabbed my shoulder and gave a little shake, "it's your fault, Jack. It was you that wanted to go up there."

What did she mean? Was she reading my mind?

"I *didn't*. I wanted to–"

"...to find Atahualpa's treasure. One story says it's up there, 'beneath the great tree that catches the first dawn'."

Chapter Eight

"You know I didn't mean it." She had me going already, and the day had hardly started.

"Relax, Jack, relax. *I* wanted to go up there. You mentioned the treasure and I thought of the legend. That's all."

"But, if it's this easy, loads of people will have gone looking already, won't they?"

"Obviously. We aren't going to *find* anything. I told you, the Spanish got it all. Come on." She headed back to the fire. "Let's get breakfast."

We got Sammy up, toasted bread, and drank mugs of some kind of herb tea. Jody had always been either bored or cocky, but now she was quiet and thoughtful. Sammy was also thinking hard – not usually one of his strong points.

As we walked, the undergrowth closed in and Jody started hacking again. I had a thought and went to walk close behind.

"You said you wanted to go up here, right?" I shouted over the swishing machete.

"Right."

"So you must have seen it, from below, with your dad?"

Hack, hack, hack. No answer.

"So why *didn't* you go?"

Hack, hack, hack. This time I just waited.

"Dad wouldn't," she said at last.

"Hang on. *Why* wouldn't he?"

Jody glanced round, then carried on.

"He didn't say."

"But..." Oh, here we went again. "Maybe it's dangerous. Maybe he knows that."

"I don't think so." The hacking slowed down, as though she was at least thinking about it. "He'd have said. There was just always someplace else he wanted to go."

"I thought you said he always does what you tell him."

Jody turned back and held out the machete. "Have a go, Jack. Just head straight up, OK."

Obviously she wanted to shut me up, but I'd been dying to try. Anyone else and I'd have asked yesterday. It was fun too. Once I got a rhythm going, the heavy blade seemed to swing itself, slicing through fleshy stems, with no resistance at all. The tangle fell aside in heaps revealing earth and roots and...

What was *this*, half hidden under the chopped stems? We'd seen butterflies and a few birds, but no animals. This must be the body of one.

They crowded up behind.

"Hey," said Sammy, "it's... What is it?"

"Oh, come *on,*" groaned Jody.

I ignored her, used the knife to clear the debris. A lizard! Quite big, probably greeny brown once, but it must have been dead a while. I prodded it with the blade.

"Stop it." Jody shouldered me aside and grabbed the machete before I could stop her. "You two – you gotta play all the time, don't you?" Why was she so angry?

Off she went, machete swinging, not looking back.

An hour passed, and the forest opened up again. There'd been no kind of view of anything since we left the camping place. There wasn't now, but I saw something I recognized. Rocky slopes reared up on either side, a steep little valley with no stream.

The place I'd dreamed about.

"Is this it?" I asked Jody.

She glanced back.

"You know, the valley, leading up to the tree?"

"How can you tell?"

I shrugged. If I mentioned my dream, she'd just make fun. "I thought we'd come far enough, that's all."

She gave me a funny, almost worried look, then led on, faster all the time, as though she couldn't wait. It was like the dream, but the long legs I saw ahead were Jody's and, instead of a slim brown back, the bulging pack with tent and cooking gear. I'd never asked her about carrying more. Just as well – it would only slow us down.

Now I was doing it too. *Anything* to go faster – and we had the whole day ahead. What was going on?

Half an hour passed. Sammy and I were breathing hard and Jody must be getting tired too, because she wasn't going quite as fast. Then suddenly, like a light going off, the pleasant green dimness of the forest was plunged into the last gloom of twilight.

Chapter Nine

Jody turned to wait for us.

"This is stupid. We're going too fast. We'll be knackered."

She was the one setting the pace, but never mind that. "What's happened?"

She was taking off the pack. "What?"

"This darkness?"

"What d'ya think? A cloud, dummy."

Jody was back to her normal rude aggressive self. But I *was* being stupid – it must have been like this when we got up, before the sun cleared the eastern hills.

As we sat sipping from plastic mineral-water bottles, I shivered. "It's cold. That can't just be a cloud, can it?"

Jody frowned, stuck a finger in her mouth and held it up.

"Wind's changed. Normally blows up from the east, the Amazon. Now it's from the west." She pointed on up the valley. "I suppose it *could* be cold air from the Andes..." She trailed to silence.

It didn't sound likely. The nearest really high mountains were miles away.

"Come on." She grabbed the pack. "Let's move, or we'll get chilled."

Always before, the damp warmth of the forest had made me sweat. Now the wind got stronger as we walked, cutting through my clothes.

"Hang on," I called to Jody. "I'm going to put my sweater on."

"Rain-gear might be better." All cockiness was gone. She really did look worried now. "Keep the wind out."

We put on our plastic ponchos and set

off again. It was hard just to keep going. The wind thrust into our faces, whipping away the breath we needed so badly. We struggled on. If Jody didn't complain with that big load, no way was I going to.

Sammy looked pale and tired, but his mouth was tight, eyes fixed in front of him, like he was obsessed. Again, it wasn't like him – not at all.

We kept close together. I huddled along, using Jody and the pack as a windbreak, and Sammy walked behind, taking shelter from us both.

The hissing of wind through trees grew to a roaring, as though we were walking beside a raging river. Then water started dripping down and I realized the noise was more than just the wind. A rainstorm was pounding on the canopy overhead and it had taken this long to get through. It hadn't rained since we arrived in Ecuador. This was supposed to be the dry season.

It started to come through for real now, huge drops which must have collected on the leaves and, every now and then, a mini-shower, as though there were monkeys up there, throwing glasses of water down on our heads. Good job we had the ponchos. A few minutes more and it was as though the whole canopy had washed away. The air was thick with water and the wind dashed it into our faces.

Jody turned, grabbed Sammy's arm. "Can't walk through this," she shouted over the uproar. She grabbed me too and pulled us towards a clump of bushes, probably the best shelter we'd find.

We put Sammy at the back, huddled under the bushes. It wasn't much drier here – like sitting in a river instead of standing in the deep end of a swimming pool – but at least we weren't being blown away. These rucksacks had better be waterproof.

"Storm like this is usually over pretty quick," Jody explained. "We'll shelter a while and... Gee, I don't know. It does rain in the dry season, but not this hard, and it's never this cold. I think..."

She was trying to say something, struggling for words. Her cheeks were red and I could see the goosebumps on her legs.

"Look," she said at last, "we gotta be sensible, guys. We gotta turn back."

No *way*, not after coming this far. I was about to say it out loud. Then I glanced at Sammy, huddled, shivering, teeth chattering from cold. I really *really* didn't want to give up, but Jody was right. We had to.

Sammy swallowed hard, pressing against me for warmth. "We *can't*."

"What?" Jody and I both said it at once.

"We have to go on. It's not far, and it's really important."

"Important? What are you talking about?" I asked him.

Sammy stared up at me, blue eyes wide, blond hair turned to dark and sodden rat-tails on his forehead.

"I can't explain. I just *know*."

Chapter Ten

Sammy was saying exactly what I felt. We *had* to go on, even though the only sensible thing was to turn back. This was way too weird.

"OK," said Jody, "we'll wait till it stops, then decide."

"Is he right?" I asked her. "*Are* we nearly there?"

The usual shrug. "We went real fast. Can't be that far."

"Another hour?"

"Less. But in *this*," she nodded at the storm, "a day, a week, maybe never. Let's get on the warmest gear we got. We'll leave the packs here. Be easier without them."

Sheltering one another as best we could, we put sweaters on and pulled the ponchos back over the top. By the time we'd finished, the wind had dropped. Water came down still, but not so much, and the roaring had faded to a hiss, like a distant sea on pebbles. Five minutes more and there was just the odd drip. And it wasn't cold any more – not at all.

Jody sighed and started pulling off the poncho and sweater again. "Crazy weather – just can't be natural."

"It's not," said Sammy.

We both stared at him.

"I mean…" he struggled to explain. "Not just the storm – everything. We *all* wanted to come up this valley, didn't we, and… Oh, I don't know what's up there, but…"

"You're right." Jody's face was set hard. "*Something* is. OK, I'm going on to take a look. You guys wait here for me."

"No way!" I wasn't staying behind and we couldn't leave Sammy.

Jody shook her head. "I'm responsible for you guys. Now – all this weird stuff – I don't *know* it's safe, not any more. I'll tell you the way down. If I'm not back in–"

"No!" I clenched my fists. Responsible! No way was some *girl* responsible for *me*. "Either we all go on–"

"No. I'm in charge." She stood with hands on hips, legs slightly apart. Always before she'd been strong and solid, diving in the river, playing volleyball, carrying the heavy pack. Now she looked fragile, as though a strong wind could blow her away like a twig. "You'll do what I say, Jack."

She stared at me, face flushed, fists clenched. For once *I'd* got to *her*. Normally I'd have thought it was a laugh, but now – oh, whatever Uncle Don said, I wasn't taking orders from an eleven-year-old.

"Think about it. You were only 'in charge' because you know this forest. Well, you've just admitted this is weird, something you *don't* know. Fine, how about *I* go ahead. You stay with Sammy." What was I saying? I wanted to go on all right, but not alone. It was just the effect she had on me and I couldn't stop myself. "Be sensible, Jody. I'm older, I'm bigger and—"

"You're a *boy*. Is that it?"

"If you like. Look..." I stopped. Her face was so dark she seemed ready to explode.

"OK, tough guy, I'll fight you for it. Winner goes up."

I couldn't believe it, not even from Jody. But there'd never be a better chance to teach her that lesson.

"What's the matter – scared?"

That did it. "Fine, come on."

I was about to beckon, but she sprang before I could move. Her rush knocked me

off balance and she hooked a leg behind mine. Nothing fancy, just playground fighting, but I slammed down on my back with Jody on top. She grabbed my wrists and shoved them into the wet grass. I bucked and struggled to get free. Sammy was pulling at her too.

"Stop it!" he yelled. "Please. Can't we all go?"

She glanced up at him. It was only because she'd rushed me, caught me by surprise, or she'd never have got me down like this. Now I just couldn't get loose.

"Please, Jody." Sammy tugged at her again. "We all saw him."

What was he talking about? I carried on struggling. "Let go! Get *off!*"

Jody freed my arms and stood up. "Saw who?" she asked Sammy. "Hey, did you have a dream last night?" So *she* must have dreamed something too.

He told her about a "scary" dream, walking up a valley, this valley, following a brown-skinned boy. My dream. The scary bit was the part I'd hardly seen, the flash of bright, then red. He didn't know what it was either.

Jody turned to me, a thoughtful look on her face, held out a hand. "Come on, Jack. Sorry if I hurt you."

I ignored the hand, scrambled up. "As if!"

She wasn't listening. "What did you dream?"

I couldn't get my mind off the fight. Just because she'd jumped me. That was all. It *had* to be. I shook my head. "Same as Sammy, more or less. What about you?"

"Real nightmare. Like you guys, but maybe I saw what you didn't. When I woke up, I thought it was just an ordinary dream. I get them sometimes – nightmares." They were both staring up the hill.

"Right," Jody went on. "We'd better do what Sammy says. Please, Jack," she didn't look round at me, "don't make trouble all the time, OK."

Me! I'd wanted to do what Sammy said, before he even said it. I'd had my chance to teach her that lesson. Oh, if *only* I'd taken it.

We left the packs behind, covered with the ponchos in case it rained again, then headed on. I was wet from my tumble in the grass, but it didn't matter now the weather was back to normal. I let Sammy follow Jody and walked along a few steps behind.

Why wouldn't she tell us about her dream? And how *had* she got me down so easily? I should have–

A sudden flash of bright colour, yellow and brick-red. A snake, more than a metre long, burst out of the undergrowth, flew at Sammy and bit him on the leg.

Chapter Eleven

Sammy crumpled to the ground, clutching his ankle and screaming. The snake was gone.

"What happened?" Jody ran back to stand over him.

I totally lost it, grabbed her arm. "You said there wouldn't *be* any snakes."

She pushed me away. "*Snakes?* Let me take a look."

Sammy screamed and screamed and – oh, what were we going to do? Miles from anywhere... nothing we *could* do and... he was going to *die*.

Jody delivered a full-arm slap across his face, knocking him flat on his back. I was *really* ready to thump her now, but something cut through my panic and held me back.

"Which leg?" she shouted in his face, then rolled jeans up and sock down. "Come on, where was it?"

Sammy lay pale-faced and sobbing, said nothing.

Jody rolled up the other jeans-leg. Then started taking off his trainers. "Where *was* it? Higher up?"

I grabbed her again. "You've got to do something."

Again she shook me off. She had both his legs bare, from toe to knee. "Calm down, Jack. You look. He hasn't been bitten."

I gritted my teeth. "The left leg," I told her, "just above the ankle."

"Look." She showed me. Nothing.

"Could it bite without leaving a mark?"

"No way."

"Come on, Sammy." I bent to his ear, struggling for calm. "Where does it hurt?"

"It... It doesn't." Tiny shaking voice. "It *did*." Much stronger now. He sat up and pointed. Exactly where I'd said.

"Could it have just got the jeans?" I asked Jody.

She shook her head. "That wouldn't

hurt. What did it look like?"

"Big, stripy, red, yellow and black."

"A *coral* snake. Where did it go?"

"I didn't see." Panic stirred again. "Is it poisonous?"

"Deadly."

"Oh, no! We have to..."

"We don't have to do *anything*, Jack. He wasn't bitten, remember. You don't *get* coral snakes up here. I wonder if there even was one."

"But I saw it."

Jody was deep in thought. "Seems to me..." She stopped.

"What?" Sammy seemed to have forgotten his shock.

"Like someone doesn't want us up here..."

"More like someone *does*..." I started.

"You're *both* right," shouted Sammy.

"So who is it – who are they?" Jody corrected herself.

Sammy shook his head, but he was

right. We'd all had the dream and we all *had* to climb the valley. That had to come from someone, maybe the boy in the dream. But the weird storm, and now this...

Jody pulled Sammy to his feet. Whether the snake was real or not, he was pale-faced, shivering, glancing at the undergrowth ahead.

"Come on," said Jody, "I'll give you a piggyback."

"No. He's *my* brother."

She shrugged and Sammy climbed up on my back. "It's OK," she told him. "No snake can get to you up there."

Sammy's no heavyweight, but I was soon struggling. Within a minute, Jody was out of sight. Sammy called for her to wait, but there was no reply.

I couldn't go any faster. "Don't worry," I said. "She'll wait." I had to stop thinking about the fight. Oh, if only she'd disappear altogether.

"It was pretty, wasn't it?" asked Sammy.

"What was?"

"The snake." He was trying to be brave.

"Prettiest snake *I've* ever seen or *thought* I've seen. Do *you* think it was real?"

"I hardly saw it," said Sammy. "I *felt* it, but... Maybe not."

We walked on in silence.

"Wasn't Jody great?" he said then. "The way she helped me."

The truth was, I'd totally lost it, while Jody had been sensible and calm. But it was too much. Here I was, *carrying* Sammy, while he told me how great *Jody* was. The ground was almost level, the trees more widely spaced. A fair amount of blue was visible above. More important, there was nothing underfoot but short and springy grass.

I put him down. "It's OK. There's nowhere here for snakes to hide."

He glanced up and managed a brave smile. "I'd like to see it again – you know, not too close. Maybe in a glass case in the zoo."

After a minute we came out into a huge clearing. Jody was staring down at something. "Come on, guys, you won't *believe* this."

Chapter Twelve

Beyond Jody was the tree. I could see all of it, the huge trunk, rising without branches for ten metres, then the mass of yellow-green foliage stretching up, it seemed, to touch the blue of the cloudless sky.

But she didn't mean that. She was pointing down at water, a lake, filling the valley ahead. "It was supposed to be here. They say the Incas dumped the treasure in a lake when the Spanish came."

The sun still wasn't high enough to light the lake. Dark, cool and mysterious, not a ripple touched its mirror surface, where a second tree plunged down to unimaginable depths.

But Sammy pointed on, beyond lake and tree. "No. It's over there – whatever it is."

"Great!" Jody scanned around. "There's no way round." She was right. The valley sides were cliffs, vertical, unclimbable, plunging straight into the lake. "And in the water..." She pointed. "Take a look."

There was no beach. The grass, smooth as a lawn, just ended, and a hand's breadth below, the water began. I went to the edge and stared down, but the bright reflection hid everything. It must be very deep or very muddy.

"Jack..." Jody's voice sounded dull and flat.

I turned to them, a sudden ringing in my ears.

"I'm..." Sammy stepped towards me, reached out, "...tired..." He took another step, slumped face-down.

My head was spinning. "Jody!"

But she was down too, asleep or unconscious.

What now? Some kind of gas from the lake maybe? Got to get them out of here. I headed for Sammy. But my legs gave way and–

I was sitting on the far side of the lake, right under the giant tree. Alone.

Someone came towards me from the valley's end. I knew him at once, a boy, about fifteen, brown skin, tall and slim, dressed in loincloth and sandals, with a gold band in his hair.

He smiled, spoke in a deep rich voice. The language was foreign, nothing I'd ever heard, and yet I understood.

"At last. I have waited so long. You are brave. You have come. Will you help me?"

I wanted to say, yes, of course I will, but I couldn't speak. It didn't seem to matter.

The boy smiled again.

"I am Huaroc of the Quiucara. I was to be leader of my clan, but my uncle led me here and brought men to kill me. He set powerful magic barriers. No one has ever found me. The cave, where I still lie," he pointed on along the valley. "It is cursed and my spirit cannot rest there. Please take me from this evil place and bury me beside my ancestors. Or else release my spirit to the air with sacred fire. Will you help?"

Again I couldn't answer. Then his face changed. "They are coming."

I tried to look round, but couldn't move any more than I could speak. The boy ran off across the grass, and a dozen men, older, bigger, dashed past and after him, with curving knives, glinting in the sun, raised up to strike.

That bright flash and the red colour in my dream. Maybe Jody had seen *all* of this in hers, but thank goodness, I managed to get my eyes closed in time.

"Jack, come on. Are you OK?"

Where was I? This darkness was quiet and peaceful and safe. I didn't want to leave it.

"Wake up, Jack." Another voice. Then something cold and shocking on my brow and neck.

"Get off!" I jerked away.

"Did you dream it? Did you dream it too?"

I opened my eyes, squinting against the brightness. I was lying where I'd fallen on the lake shore.

"Did you dream?" asked Sammy. "Jody and I had the same one."

He told me. It was the same as mine. What had the boy meant by "powerful magic barriers"? The storm? The snake? Maybe this lake too? It didn't matter. Nothing was going to stop me now. "Come on." I scrambled up. "We'll have to swim across."

Jody frowned, nodded towards the

water. "Take another look."

I went to stare into the depths. In minutes the sun would top the trees behind us and light this gloomy lake.

"Over there!" Sammy pointed.

A sunbeam had found its way through the branches, shining like a searchlight deep into the water. It wasn't muddy. I could see the bottom, eight or ten metres down. *That* could be mud. Then the small bright patch went dark, as something huge swam across, cutting off the sunlight.

Chapter Thirteen

Sammy gasped. "Is it a piranha?"

"Piranhas are smaller than that," said Jody. "They live in rivers down in the rainforest. I doubt you'd get them up here."

I took another look. Lots of them down there, really huge, more Jaws than piranha. But shaped like thick and tapering barrels. "Could they be pacus?" Something I'd seen in Bristol Zoo.

Jody looked at me. "How would I know? Do I *look* like a fisherman?"

The ones at the zoo had shared a tank

with smaller fish. "If they are," I told her, "I don't think they're carnivorous."

"Fair enough." She sat down, started taking her boots off.

Not again. "Look, hang on," I said. "This time I have to go."

"Yeah, right." She got boots and socks off. "Big strong boy again? Remember what happened last time, Jack."

"Nothing *happened*…" I stopped myself. "Listen. Swimming's my thing. I train three times a week. This lake is what, twenty metres across? I can do that in under twenty seconds. I'll be out before they even smell me – or whatever fish do."

Jody sighed. "OK, big hero." She watched me take off my trainers. "I don't train three times a week. Bet I could beat you, just the same."

I paid no attention, stepped out of my jeans and pulled the T-shirt over my head. I did a racing dive. I didn't want to get any closer to the fish than I had to, so I surfaced quickly and swam hard. Perfect chance to show Jody I could do *something* really well.

But what was happening? I should be halfway across, but I was just a few metres out, making no progress at all. I swam harder – at least it felt like I was swimming, but something was stopping me, holding me in place.

Oh no! If I thrashed like this, but didn't move, it would draw those fish from every corner of the lake. Something brushed my leg. I could see it in my mind, jaws gaping wide, full of sharp teeth.

I panicked, flailing wildly, desperate to escape. But I was exhausted, limbs like stones. And the water was rising, engulfing whirling arms and kicking legs, covering my back and face and head.

Sucking me down into the deep.

Chapter Fourteen

Something brushed my *arm* now. I screamed, got a mouthful of water, tried to twist away. But this was no fish. It was holding on, pulling me up, getting my head above water.

"Cool it!" Jody's voice, right in my ear. If I didn't, *she* was going to life-save *me*.

Trying to swim wasn't helping, so I blanked out thoughts of jaws and teeth, turned on my back and floated, gasping precious air.

Jody let go. "Hey, do you believe this? It's OK going back. Hold on, Jack, I'll get you to–"

"It's OK. I'm fine." I started a gentle back crawl, reached the bank in a few strokes. Jody was out already. She offered a hand but I ignored it, forced tired limbs to haul myself up and collapsed on the grass.

"What now?" asked Sammy.

I gasped more lungfuls of air, and glanced up in time to see Jody dive back in. What was she *doing*? She *knew* we couldn't swim across.

And why didn't she surface?

Sammy grabbed my arm. "Is she OK?"

I struggled to my feet. Then she appeared, right beside the far bank, vaulted out and turned to wave. "Come on, you guys. Underwater it's OK."

I looked at Sammy, who's not that great a swimmer.

"I don't think I can, not underwater."

"We can go together if you like, hold hands." But it wouldn't be smart and I was relieved when he shook his head.

"It's OK," he told me. "I'll wait here. You go."

"Are you sure?" He'd be OK. We could keep an eye on him from over there, get back here in seconds if need be.

Sammy nodded. "Go on. Go and help Jody."

I dived in, down deep, then forward, right past the dark bulk of a fish. I ignored it and it didn't seem any more interested in me. I swam on. Jody was right, no problem at all.

But I felt as though I was bursting. It wasn't just the breath I was holding inside. Even this, the one thing I'm really good at. Even here, Jody was the one to get us through. How could I be so useless? It should have been great, swimming down here with these giant fish, but I felt as if I was dissolving in a bath of acid bitterness.

I reached the bank and broke the surface. Jody crouched above, smiling, reaching down.

I'd given up. I took her hand, let her haul me out and set me on the bank, sat beside her, getting my breath back.

I'd thought I was a decent athlete, but I could never compete with Jody. She was a natural, did everything really well, almost without trying. She had no idea about fighting, but it was no accident she'd got me down so quickly. Good job Sammy was there to break us up.

I sighed. For all I knew she'd beat me in a swimming race as well. So much for girls being weak. So much for them being useless at sport.

She squeezed my arm. "Come on, it's only 'cause you went first."

"What is?"

"Couldn't miss it from the bank. Underwater, you went fine, but when you surfaced – *really* weird – you just stopped dead. If I'd gone first, *you'd* have seen it." This was the first time she'd shown any sign of caring about how I felt.

I had a thought. "How did you know we'd be able to swim back?"

She didn't answer.

Of course, she *hadn't* known. We could have been stuck out there. Those fish could have been killers. She hadn't known and yet she hadn't even hesitated.

She'd risked her life.

For me.

Jody was a pain all right, but right now I wouldn't swap her for anyone I knew.

"Thanks, Jody," I told her. "That was really brave."

"Come *on*." She blushed and turned away. "Hey, I couldn't just leave you out there, right?"

We went on to the dark and rocky hole, gaping in the angle where the canyon walls met. From far away, the tree had seemed important, but now it was this cave that mattered. And the boy in the dream had called it an evil place.

Jody stopped. "After you."

I stared at her. Was she nervous too? Not very Jody-like. "Hey," I forced a grin. "What happened to the big strong girl always going first?"

She grinned back. "We know what's in there, right? Actually I'm not that keen – you know, dead things."

Of *course*. That lizard. I stared at Jody. For the first time she actually needed me to do something. "Hey, no one's perfect," Jody pointed out. "Get in there. Unless *you–*"

"No, no problem." But after about five steps I realized there was. The cave turned hard left and whatever was underfoot was way too sharp and uneven for bare feet in darkness.

I reported back. "We need shoes," left on the far bank, "and torches," down the hill in the packs.

We headed for the lakeside but long before we reached it I realized. There was no bright splash of orange over there.

Sammy had disappeared.

Chapter Fifteen

I sprinted for the lake. Jody must have noticed at the same moment, because we ran side by side, hitting the water in racing dives. I didn't go deep – it had been OK in this direction. A few seconds to cross and, by the end, I was a metre ahead. Any other time I'd have been relieved that I could beat her at *something*. Now, of course, nothing mattered but Sammy.

I scrambled out and grabbed my shoes. He wouldn't have gone back, not after seeing that snake. Why would he anyway? Someone must have taken him.

Shoes on, we ran together down the valley – and met Sammy, strolling up towards us, his small pack on his back.

"You *stupid*..." I stood over him, my fear turned instantly to fury. "What were you *doing*?"

"You need torches and stuff, don't you? I thought, while you were exploring, I'd go down and fetch them."

"Lighten up, Jack," said Jody. "Nice one, Sammy."

"OK, I *suppose*." Why was I yelling? He was right, and he'd been pretty brave to go down past where we'd seen the snake.

Back at the lakeside, Jody unpacked. "What are these for?" She held up candles and matches.

"Remember the dream," said Sammy. "What he wanted."

"*Burn* him." Jody made a face. "Couldn't we take him down with us? It'll just be bones by now, won't it?" The face again. She really didn't like this stuff. "He said 'beside his ancestors'. Maybe we can find out where the Quiucaras used to bury people."

I thought about it. "If we take a skeleton down, they may want to put him in a museum or something."

"Good point." Jody made a bundle: torches, matches, candles and shoes, tied up tight in layer over layer of poly-bags. She lashed it round my waist and the two of us swam back through the depths of the lake.

Everything stayed dry. I went into the cave alone, while Jody gathered firewood.

Even with the torch, this place had a damp and creepy feel, as though my skin was crawling with a million tiny slugs. Clothes would have been nice, but I wasn't going back again.

A few metres in, the cave widened to a large chamber. I flashed the torch around and saw something pale, streaked with red. It *couldn't* be! I yelled, jumped back, stumbled and dropped the torch.

Chapter Sixteen

Luckily, the torch didn't go out. I grabbed it and headed back to get Jody.

Then I stopped. What was I *doing*? I had a problem so I headed straight to Jody to solve it for me. And what I'd seen up there – thought I'd seen – was just about perfect to freak her totally.

I went back to the chamber. Even now I was prepared, it still wasn't easy to look at this: a body, the boy from our dreams, very pale in death, mouth open, eyes staring.

I moved the light away. He'd been dead hundreds of years. This must be an illusion, another of his uncle's magic barriers. I left the torch on the ground, pointing the other way and inched forward, eyes closed, feeling with the toe of my trainer.

"Everything OK?" Jody's shout made me jump.

"Fine." I tried to sound cool.

At that moment, my foot touched something, a stone maybe, certainly not heavy like a body. I reached down. It felt like a dry bone. I took it back to the torch. It *was* a bone, broken, maybe human. I shone the light around again.

No body now, and the cave felt less threatening. But, oh, it was so sad. That boy in the dream had been so young and strong. Just to be killed like that and forgotten all this time. Now there was nothing left but these white bones.

I'd brought poly-bags and I gathered up every bone, every fragment. It was fine now, as though Huaroc was here, alive, somehow letting me know how glad he was. I was glad too, glad we could do *something* for this poor guy. Even though it was so little and so very late.

The fire was blazing, right on the lakeshore. The bones, light and dry with age, fell to powder in the glowing depths. I sat feeding them in, while Sammy watched from across the water and Jody brought more wood. When she'd piled up more than we could possibly use, she stretched out beside me, letting her sodden clothes dry in the sun.

We sat in silence for a while. Then Jody looked sideways at the skull – all that was left of Huaroc now. "We ought to say something."

"Like what?"

The familiar shrug. "Goodbye, Huaroc of the Quiucara. We hope you're at peace now."

I thrust the skull into the hottest depths of the fire.

Chapter Seventeen

"It's kind of – different now." Sammy smiled up at me. "You know?"

I shifted the heavy pack on my back. Jody reckoned we should be used to the altitude by now. Before we set off, she'd repacked, giving Sammy the cooking pots and me all kinds of stuff. A few metres ahead of us, leading on down the valley, she looked like a normal hiker instead of a walking junk-pile.

But Sammy didn't mean that.

"What is?"

"Everything. You *know*." He pointed

back the way we'd come.

I glanced back. This was one of the few places where we could see through to the big tree. That was what he meant. Something that big would always look amazing, but it didn't seem special now – not like before. Nor did this valley, which meant we'd done it: Huaroc was at rest, for sure.

Without Jody's strength and courage and determination, we'd never have made it. That stuff she'd said, about going to Cambridge and making piles of money – I'd thought it was just boasting, but if this girl set out to do something, who could ever stop her?

"Hey, Jody."

She turned to wait for us.

"Listen. When you make your first million, I'll let you treat me to dinner at the Ritz in London. Deal?" I held out a hand.

She smiled and grasped it. "You're on. Champagne, caviar, the lot. I'd give it, oh, about fifteen years."

The rest of the holiday was brilliant. Uncle Don drove us all around and we saw loads of cool things. We practised volleyball every day till we could give the local kids a decent game, and went for two more forest treks.

Jody's coming over for Christmas. Uncle Don phoned Dad, and Mum's fixing up interviews for her at some boarding schools near where we live. That way she'll be able to stay with us at weekends and half-terms. We've got plenty of room in our house.

About the author

What I love best is travelling – after writing books, of course! Whenever I'm on a journey, I always look for interesting places where the characters I write about can live out their adventures. You can't find much better than the cool high mountain jungles of Ecuador, alive with birds and flowers, half-seen animals, rushing water and wandering clouds. And the memories of the Indian people who lived there for centuries before the Spanish came to South America.

I'd like to thank some of those who helped me with the book: Myriam Jaramillo of Hospedaje Camino Real in Otavalo and Jens Wueller of Cabanas Indillama in Rio Verde, both of whom also provided wonderful places to stay; also Dr Maria Elena Barragan of the Quito Vivarium, who advised on Andean snakes.